SLOPPY JOE

by Dave Keane

illustrated by Denise Brunkus

SCHOLASTIC INC.
New York Toronto London Auckland
Sydney Mexico City New Delhi Hong Kong

For my six sloppy brothers—Bird, T-Roll, Crust, Snowy, Gumby, and Slim
—D.K.

For Rosemary—a neat inspiration
—D.B.

ISBN 978-0-545-28400-4

12 11 10 9 8 7 6 5 4 3 2 1   10 11 12 13 14 15/0

Printed in the U.S.A.   40

First Scholastic printing, September 2010

Typography by Jeanne L. Hogle

Mom says I'm the first kid in history to take a school picture with gum stuck in his hair.

You can barely notice.

My room looks a little bit messy,
but I know exactly where everything is . . .

. . . everything except my bearded dragon, a few of his
crickets, and a grilled cheese sandwich I lost last summer.

When you're sloppy, people are always telling you what to do.

I'd rather be raised by alligators.

I've always been good at being sloppy.

I slurp, spill, slouch, talk with my mouth full, and
put my elbows on the table without even trying.

Dad says I'm a natural.

So do Grammy and Big Grandpa.

They spread newspapers all around me
when we eat dinner at their house.

How did they know a meatball could roll that far?

But I'm not just good at being sloppy. . . .

I can catch more frogs than any kid on my street.

Just ask my mom.

I know how to help my dad in the yard.

And I'm really good at baseball because I practice, practice, practice.

But sometimes I wish I wasn't so sloppy. . . .

Like when my friend's mom doesn't let me come in the house.
"Just wait here. I'll send Jimmy out," she says.

But I wiped my feet!

"What kind of pet does the sun have?

A hot dog!"

"Hey, Mom, what did the taco say to the burrito?

Where have you bean?"

When being sloppy gets me in really big trouble, I just try out my newest jokes.

Sometimes even my best jokes
don't work.

So I decide something has to change.

That's when I make up my mind to not be sloppy anymore.

Starting tomorrow, I'll be Neat Joe.

The next day, I give the dog a shower.

I clean my room. I find that lost grilled cheese sandwich.
It's so hard I almost break my teeth.

I set the table for dinner.
I even find one of my lost crickets.

This being-neat stuff isn't as hard as I thought it would be.
But nobody cares about all my neatness because . . .

. . . everyone in my family has the flu.

I tell them not to panic. This is a job for Neat Joe.

So I bring cold socks for their foreheads.
I cover everything with germ spray.
I even make soup.

I try to cheer them up, but my jokes only make them groan louder.

"Hey, guys, what kind of dog wins every contest? A wiener dog."

Get it? Wieeeeeeeeeeener dog! What's wrong with you people?

By the time Grammy gets here,
I have everything under control.

"So what do you think of the new
Neat Joe?" I ask my family.

"He reminds me of the old Sloppy Joe," Dad says.
"And he's a very special kid," Mom says.